THIS WHOLE TOOTH FAIRY THING'S NOTHING BUT A BIG RIP-OFF!

by Lois G. Grambling
Illustrated by Thomas Payne

MARSHALL CAVENDISH • NEW YORK

Marshall Cavendish, 99 White Plains Road, Tarrytown, NY 10591
Library of Congress Cataloging-in-Publication Data
Grambling, Lois G.
This whole Tooth Fairy thing's nothing but a big rip-off! / Lois G. Grambling ; illustrated by Thomas Payne.
p. cm.
Summary: Little Hippo waits eagerly for the arrival of the Tooth Fairy and ends up making a final
tooth-to-coin exchange for her.
ISBN 0-7614-5104-8
[1. Tooth Fairy—Fiction. 2. Hippopotamus—Fiction.]   I. Payne, Thomas, ill. II. Title.
PZ7.G7655 Th 2002   [E]—dc21   2001028286

The text of this book is set in 14 point Leawood Book.
The illustrations are rendered in oils on illustration board.
Printed in Hong Kong

First edition

1 3 5 6 4 2

For Lara and Ty
who always looked forward with much anticipation
to the Tooth Fairy's visits.

— L. G. G.

Little Hippo should have been asleep.
But he wasn't.
His loose front tooth had fallen out that day.
And he was checking under his pillow to make sure it was still there.
It was.
Little Hippo hoped size counted with the Tooth Fairy.
Little Hippo could hear rain hitting against the roof.
"I hope the Tooth Fairy remembered her umbrella tonight," he said turning off his light
She hadn't.

The Tooth Fairy was getting wet.

Very wet.

"Drat!" she said shaking her wings.

"I should have checked the weather channel before I left."

The Tooth Fairy looked at her watch.

(Fortunately, it was waterproof!)

"Nearly eleven," she said. "And I still have two more deliveries to make. This rain is ruining my schedule. Not to mention my outfit!! And my hairdo!!!"

Wings are not easy to flutter when they are wet.

Not even fairy wings.

The Tooth Fairy was getting tired.

And . . . Ah—Choo!

She seemed to be catching a cold.

The Tooth Fairy was DEFINITELY not a happy fairy tonight!

But she had a job to do.

Checking her list she headed for Little Hippo's house.

The rain pounding hard against Little Hippo's roof woke him up.
He turned on the light.
It was after eleven.
"The Tooth Fairy should have been here by now!" he said reaching
under his pillow.
Little Hippo couldn't believe it!
His big front tooth was still there!
He reached under his pillow . . . again.
No shiny big coin!
No shiny little coin!
Not even a paper I. O. U.!

Little Hippo was mad!

"This whole Tooth Fairy thing's nothing but a big rip-off!!" he yelled.

The Tooth Fairy, coming in for a landing, heard him.

She couldn't help but hear him.

Now it was her turn to be mad.

She flew in Little Hippo's window and splashed down on his bed.

"If this whole Tooth Fairy thing's nothing but a big rip-off," she said,
"then who am I?

Santa Claus?!

Or maybe the Easter Bunny?!

And why am I flying around on such a miserable night?!

Wearing this unbelievable outfit?!

Ah—Choo!

Catching a cold . . .

Doing this tooth-for-coin exchange thing?!"

Little Hippo's eyes opened wide.

"There really is a Tooth Fairy!!" he said.

"You bet your bottom molars there is!" the Tooth Fairy said.

"And you're looking at her!"

"But I thought no one ever got to see the Tooth Fairy," Little Hippo
said.

"Usually no one does!" the Tooth Fairy said. "But after hearing what
you just yelled, I thought maybe you needed to."

"You do see me, don't you, Little Hippo?"

"I do!" said Little Hippo.

"At least that's a beginning!" said the Tooth Fairy.

The Tooth Fairy looked out the window.

It was still raining

"I wish I didn't have to go out again tonight," she said.

"But I have one more exchange to make."

"Who?" asked Little Hippo.

"Cub Bear in the woods beyond town. You wouldn't want to make that exchange for me, would you?"

"Not really," Little Hippo said looking out at the rain.

"Besides, my bike has a flat."

"Suppose you could fly?" the Tooth Fairy asked.

"Get real, Tooth Fairy" Little Hippo said. "Hippos can't fly!"

The Tooth Fairy pulled off her wings and stuck them on Little Hippo.
"You can now!" she said.
Little Hippo's eyes opened wide.
"What holds them on?" he asked. "Fairy magic?"
"Superglue," said the Tooth Fairy.

"But I don't know how to make wings work," Little Hippo said.

"It's easy," said the Tooth Fairy.

"Just flutter.

Fast.

And jump."

And that's what Little Hippo did.

And he flew right out the window!

"Hey! Don't forget these!" the Tooth Fairy yelled tossing Little Hippo a pouch marked TEETH.

And a pouch marked COINS.

Little Hippo caught them.

And put them on.

"Does tooth size count?" he asked.

"All teeth are exchanged at the same rate," the Tooth Fairy answered.

"Rats!" said Little Hippo thinking about that big tooth under his pillow.

With Little Hippo off and flying the Tooth Fairy headed over to his bed.
And fell sound asleep.
Little Hippo had never flown before.

Except in an airplane when he visited Grandma and Grandpa Hippo.
But he took to flying like a duck takes to water,
And in spite of the rain he was having a wonderful time.

When Little Hippo reached Cub Bear's house he did the tooth-for-coin exchange thing.

Then as he was getting ready to leave Cub Bear opened his eyes.

And saw him.

"Thanks, Tooth Fairy," he said.

Not knowing what else to say, Little Hippo said, "You're welcome."

Flying out the window Little Hippo heard a strange sound.
It was the Tooth Fairy.
Snoring.

ZZZ

Little Hippo followed the snores back to his house and
thumped to a landing next to his bed.

The Tooth Fairy woke up.
She looked rested.
And she wasn't sneezing.
"How did everything go?" she asked.
"Great," said Little Hippo. "Except . . ."
"Except what?" the Tooth Fairy asked.
"Except tonight," Little Hippo answered, "Cub Bear thought I was the Tooth Fairy."
"Well," the Tooth Fairy said smiling, "tonight, for him, you were. Thanks for helping."
"Any time!" said Little Hippo.

Little Hippo handed the Tooth Fairy her wings.

She put them on.

"Can I ask you something before I leave, Little Hippo?" she said.

"Ask away," said Little Hippo.

"Do you still think this Tooth Fairy thing's nothing but a big rip-off?"

Wanting to be certain of his answer before he gave it, Little Hippo
hurried over to his bed . . .

reached under his pillow . . .

and pulled out the biggest shiniest coin he had ever seen!

"No way!" he said happily.

"I'm glad," said the Tooth Fairy.

"So am I," said Little Hippo.

The rain had stopped.

The Tooth Fairy was glad about that, too.

She climbed onto the windowsill and revved up her wings.

"Can I ask you something before you leave, Tooth Fairy?" Little Hippo said.

"Ask away," said the Tooth Fairy.

"Do you ever see Santa Claus?"

"Occasionally on business," the Tooth Fairy said.

"Next time you see him," Little Hippo said, "will you tell him if he starts sneezing on Christmas Eve, I'll make his deliveries for him."

"I'll tell him," the Tooth Fairy said flying out the window.

"Don't forget," Little Hippo shouted after her.

"I won't," the Tooth Fairy shouted back.

And she didn't.

And Little Hippo Knew she didn't because . . .
On Christmas Eve he got a call from the
North Pole.
And it wasn't from the Easter Bunny!